D0204868

The MAGIC PUDDING

Written and Illustrated by

NORMAN LINDSAY

DOVER PUBLICATIONS, INC.
Mineola, New York

Bibliographical Note

This Dover edition, first published in 2006, is an unabridged republication of the work published by Angus and Robertson, Ltd., Sydney, Australia, in 1918.

International Standard Book Number: 0-486-45281-6

Manufactured in the United States of America
Dover Publications, Inc., 31 East 2nd Street, Mineola, N.Y. 11501

First Slice

THIS is a frontways view of Bunyip Bluegum and his Uncle Wattleberry. At a glance you can see what a fine, round, splendid fellow Bunyip Bluegum is, without me telling you. At a second glance you can see that the Uncle is more square than round, and that his face has whiskers on it.

Looked at sideways you can still see what a splendid fellow Bunyip is, though you can only see one of his Uncle's whiskers.

Observed from behind, however, you completely lose sight of the whiskers, and so fail to realize how immensely important they are. In fact, these very whiskers

were the chief cause of Bunyip's leaving home to see the world, for, as he often said to himself –

> 'Whiskers alone are bad enough
> Attached to faces coarse and rough;
> But how much greater their offence is
> When stuck on Uncles' countenances.'

The plain truth was that Bunyip and his Uncle lived in a small house in a tree, and there was no room for the whiskers. What was worse, the whiskers were red, and they blew about in the wind, and Uncle Wattleberry would insist on bringing them to the dinner table with him, where they got in the soup.

Bunyip Bluegum was a tidy bear, and he objected to whisker soup, so he was forced to eat his meals outside, which was awkward, and besides, lizards came and borrowed his soup.

His Uncle refused to listen to reason on the subject of his whiskers. It was quite useless giving him hints, such as presents of razors, and scissors, and boxes of matches to burn them off. On such occasions he would remark –

'Shaving may add an air that's somewhat brisker,
For dignity, commend me to the whisker.'

Or, when more deeply moved, he would exclaim –

'As noble thoughts the inward being grace,
So noble whiskers dignify the face.'

Prayers and entreaties to remove the whiskers being of no avail, Bunyip decided to leave home without more ado.

The trouble was that he couldn't make up his mind whether to be a Traveller or a Swagman. You can't go about the world being nothing, but if you are a traveller you have to carry a bag, while if you are a swagman you

have to carry a swag, and the question is: Which is the heavier?

At length he decided to put the matter before Egbert Rumpus Bumpus, the poet, and ask his advice. He found Egbert busy writing poems on a slate. He was so busy that he only had time to sing out –

> 'Don't interrupt the poet, friend,
> Until his poem's at an end.'

and went on writing harder than ever. He wrote all down one side of the slate and all up the other, and then remarked –

> 'As there's no time to finish that,
> The time has come to have our chat.
> Be quick, my friend, your business state,
> Before I take another slate.'

'The fact is,' said the Bunyip, 'I have decided to see the world, and I cannot make up my mind whether to be a Traveller or a Swagman. Which would you advise?'

Then said the Poet –

> 'As you've no bags it's plain to see
> A traveller you cannot be;
> And as a swag you haven't either
> You cannot be a swagman neither.
> For travellers must carry bags,
> And swagmen have to hump their swags
>   Like bottle-ohs or ragmen.
> As you have neither swag nor bag
> You must remain a simple wag,
>   And not a swag- or bagman.'

'Dear me,' said Bunyip Bluegum, 'I never thought of that. What must I do in order to see the world without carrying swags or bags?'

The Poet thought deeply, put on his eyeglass, and said impressively –

> 'Take my advice, don't carry bags,
> For bags are just as bad as swags;
>   They're never made to measure.
> To see the world, your simple trick
> Is but to take a walking-stick –

Assume an air of pleasure,
And tell the people near and far
You stroll about because you are
A Gentleman of Leisure.'

'You have solved the problem,' said Bunyip Bluegum, and, wringing his friend's hand, he ran straight home, took his Uncle's walking-stick, and assuming an air of pleasure, set off to see the world.

He found a great many things to see, such as dandelions, and ants, and traction engines, and bolting horses, and furniture being removed, besides being kept busy raising his hat, and passing the time of day with people on the road, for he was a very well-bred young fellow, polite in his manners, graceful in his attitudes, and able to converse on a great variety of subjects, having read all the best Australian poets.

Unfortunately, in the hurry of leaving home, he had

forgotten to provide himself with food, and at lunch time found himself attacked by the pangs of hunger.

'Dear me,' he said, 'I feel quite faint. I had no idea that one's stomach was so important. I have everything I require, except food; but without food everything is rather less than nothing.

> 'I've got a stick to walk with.
> I've got a mind to think with.
> I've got a voice to talk with.
> I've got an eye to wink with.
> I've lots of teeth to eat with,
> A brand new hat to bow with,
> A pair of fists to beat with,
> A rage to have a row with.
> No joy it brings
>   To have indeed
> A lot of things
>   One does not need.
> Observe my doleful plight.
>   For here am I without a crumb
>   To satisfy a raging tum –
> O what an oversight!'

As he was indulging in these melancholy reflexions he came round a bend in the road, and discovered two people in the very act of having lunch. These people were none other than Bill Barnacle, the sailor, and his friend, Sam Sawnoff, the penguin bold.

Bill was a small man with a large hat, a beard half as large as his hat, and feet half as large as his beard. Sam Sawnoff's feet were sitting down and his body was standing up, because his feet were so short and his body so long that he had to do both together. They had a pudding in a basin, and the smell that arose from it was so delightful that Bunyip Bluegum was quite unable to pass on.

'Excuse me,' he said, raising his hat, 'but am I right in supposing that this is a steak-and-kidney pudding?'

'At present it is,' said Bill Barnacle.

'It smells delightful,' said Bunyip Bluegum.

'It is delightful,' said Bill, eating a large mouthful.

Bunyip Bluegum was too much of a gentleman to invite himself to lunch, but he said carelessly, 'Am I right in supposing that there are onions in this pudding?'

Before Bill could reply, a thick, angry voice came out of the pudding, saying –

> 'Onions, bunions, corns and crabs,
> Whiskers, wheels and hansom cabs,
> Beef and bottles, beer and bones,
> Give him a feed and end his groans.'

'Albert, Albert,' said Bill to the Puddin', 'where's your manners?'

'Where's yours?' said the Puddin' rudely, 'guzzling away there, and never so much as offering this stranger a slice.'

'There you are,' said Bill. 'There's nothing this Puddin' enjoys more than offering slices of himself to strangers.'

'How very polite of him,' said Bunyip, but the Puddin' replied loudly –

> 'Politeness be sugared, politeness be hanged,
> Politeness be jumbled and tumbled and banged.
> It's simply a matter of putting on pace,
> Politeness has nothing to do with the case.'

'Always anxious to be eaten,' said Bill, 'that's this Puddin's mania. Well, to oblige him, I ask you to join us at lunch.'

'Delighted, I'm sure,' said Bunyip, seating himself. 'There's nothing I enjoy more than a good go in at steak-and-kidney pudding in the open air.'

'Well said,' remarked Sam Sawnoff, patting him on the back. 'Hearty eaters are always welcome.'

'You'll enjoy this Puddin',' said Bill, handing him a large slice. 'This is a very rare Puddin'.'

'It's a cut-an'-come-again Puddin',' said Sam.

'It's a Christmas, steak, and apple-dumpling Puddin',' said Bill.

'It's a – Shall I tell him?' he asked, looking at Bill. Bill nodded, and the Penguin leaned across to Bunyip Bluegum and said in a low voice, 'It's a Magic Puddin'.'

'No whispering,' shouted the Puddin' angrily. 'Speak up. Don't strain a Puddin's ears at the meal table.'

'No harm intended, Albert,' said Sam, 'I was merely remarking how well the crops are looking. Call him Albert when addressing him,' he added to Bunyip Bluegum. 'It soothes him.'

'I am delighted to make your acquaintance, Albert,' said Bunyip.

'No soft soap from total strangers,' said the Puddin', rudely.

'Don't take no notice of him, mate,' said Bill. 'That's only his rough and ready way. What this Puddin' requires is politeness and constant eatin'.'

They had a delightful meal, eating as much as possible, for whenever they stopped eating the Puddin' sang out –

'Eat away, chew away, munch and bolt and guzzle,
Never leave the table till you're full up to the muzzle.'

But at length they had to stop, in spite of these encouraging remarks, and, as they refused to eat any more, the Puddin' got out of his basin, remarking – 'If you won't eat any more here's giving you a run for the sake of exercise', and he set off so swiftly on a pair of extremely thin legs that Bill had to run like an antelope to catch him up.

'My word,' said Bill, when the Puddin' was brought back. 'You have to be as smart as paint to keep this Puddin' in order. He's that artful, lawyers couldn't manage him. Put your hat on, Albert, like a little gentleman,' he added, placing the basin on his head. He took the Puddin's hand, Sam took the other, and they all set off along the road. A peculiar thing about the Puddin' was that, though they had all had a great many slices off him, there was no sign of the place whence the slices had been cut.

'That's where the Magic comes in,' explained Bill. 'The more you eats the more you gets. Cut-an'-come-again is his name, an' cut, an' come again, is his nature.

Me an' Sam has been eatin' away at this Puddin' for years, and there's not a mark on him. Perhaps,' he added, 'you would like to hear how we came to own this remarkable Puddin'.'

'Nothing would please me more,' said Bunyip Bluegum.

'In that case,' said Bill, 'let her go for a song.'

'Ho, the cook of the *Saucy Sausage*,
  Was a feller called Curry and Rice,
A son of a gun as fat as a tun
With a face as round as a hot-cross bun,
  Or a barrel, to be precise.

'One winter's morn we rounds the Horn,
  A-rollin' homeward bound.
We strikes on the ice, goes down in a trice,
And all on board but Curry and Rice
  And me an' Sam is drowned.

19

'For Sam an' me an' the cook, yer see,
   We climbs on a lump of ice,
And there in the sleet we suffered a treat
For several months from frozen feet,
With nothin' at all but ice to eat,
   And ice does not suffice.

'And Sam and me we couldn't agree
   With the cook at any price.
We was both as thin as a piece of tin
While that there cook was busting his skin
   On nothin' to eat but ice.

'Says Sam to me, "It's a mystery
   More deep than words can utter;
Whatever we do, here's me an' you,
Us both as thin as Irish stoo,
   While he's as fat as butter."

'But late one night we wakes in fright
   To see by a pale blue flare,
That cook has got in a phantom pot
A big plum-duff an' a rump-steak hot,
And the guzzlin' wizard is eatin' the lot,
   On top of the iceberg bare.'

'There's a verse left out here,' said Bill, stopping the
song, 'owin' to the difficulty of explainin' exactly what
happened when me and Sam discovered the deceitful
nature of that cook. The next verse is as follows –

'Now Sam an' me can never agree
   What happened to Curry and Rice.
The whole affair is shrouded in doubt,
For the night was dark and the flare went out,
And all we heard was a startled shout,
Though I think meself, in the subsequent rout,
That us bein' thin, an' him bein' stout,
In the middle of pushin' an' shovin' about,
   He – MUST HAVE FELL OFF THE ICE.'

'That won't do, you know,' began the Puddin', but Sam said hurriedly, 'It was very dark, and there's no sayin' at this date what happened.'

'Yes there is,' said the Puddin', 'for I had my eye on the whole affair, and it's my belief that if he hadn't been so round you'd have never rolled him off the iceberg, for you was both singin' out

"Yo heave Ho" for half an hour, an' him trying to hold on to Bill's beard.'

'In the haste of the moment,' said Bill, 'he may have got a bit of a shove, for the ice bein' slippy, and us bein' justly enraged, and him bein' as round as a barrel, he may, as I said, have been too fat to save himself from rollin' off the iceberg. The point, however, is immaterial to our story, which concerns this Puddin'; and this Puddin',' said Bill patting him on the basin, 'was the very Puddin' that Curry and Rice invented on the iceberg.'

'He must have been a very clever cook,' said Bunyip.

'He was, poor feller, he was,' said Bill, greatly affected. 'For plum duff or Irish stoo there wasn't his equal in the land. But enough of these sad subjects. Pausin' only to explain that me an' Sam got off the iceberg on a homeward bound chicken coop, landed on Tierra del Fuego, walked to Valparaiso, and so got home, I will proceed to enliven the occasion with "The Ballad of the Bo'sun's Bride".'

And without more ado, Bill, who had one of those beef-and-thunder voices, roared out –

> 'Ho, aboard the *Salt Junk Sarah*
>   We was rollin' homeward bound,
> When the bo'sun's bride fell over the side
>   And very near got drowned.
> Rollin' home, rollin' home,
> Rollin' home across the foam,
>   She had to swim to save her glim
> And catch us rollin' home.'

It was a very long song, so the rest of it is left out here, but there was a great deal of rolling and roaring in it, and they all joined in the chorus. They were all singing away at the top of their pipe, as Bill called it, when round a bend in the road they came on two low-looking persons hiding behind a tree. One was a Possum, with one of those sharp, snooting, snouting sort of faces, and the other was a bulbous, boozy-looking Wombat in an old long-tailed coat, and a hat that marked him down as a man you couldn't trust in the fowlyard. They were busy sharpening up a carving knife on a portable grindstone, but the moment they caught sight of the travellers the Possum whipped the knife behind him and the Wombat put his hat over the grindstone.

Bill Barnacle flew into a passion at these signs of treachery.

'I see you there,' he shouted.

'You can't see all of us,' shouted the Possum, and the Wombat added, ''Cause why, some of us is behind the tree.'

Bill led the others aside, in order to hold a consultation.

'What on earth's to be done?' he said.

'We shall have to fight them, as usual,' said Sam.

'Why do you have to fight them?' asked Bunyip Bluegum.

'Because they're after our Puddin',' said Bill.

'They're after our Puddin',' explained Sam, 'because they're professional puddin'-thieves.'

'And as we're perfessional Puddin'-owners,' said Bill, 'we have to fight them on principle. The fighting,' he added, 'is a mere flea-bite, as the sayin' goes. The trouble is, what's to be done with the Puddin'?'

'While you do the fighting,' said Bunyip bravely, 'I shall mind the Puddin'.'

'The trouble is,' said Bill, 'that this is a very secret,

crafty Puddin', an' if you wasn't up to his game he'd be askin' you to look at a spider an' then run away while your back is turned.'

'That's right,' said the Puddin', gloomily. 'Take a Puddin's character away. Don't mind his feelings.'

'We don't mind your feelin's, Albert,' said Bill. 'What we minds is your treacherous 'abits.' But Bunyip

Bluegum said, 'Why not turn him upside-down and sit on him?'

'What a brutal suggestion,' said the Puddin'; but no notice was taken of his objections, and as soon as he was turned safely upside-down, Bill and Sam ran straight at the puddin'-thieves and commenced sparring up at them with the greatest activity.

'Put 'em up, ye puddin'-snatchers,' shouted Bill. 'Don't keep us sparrin' up here all day. Come out an' take your gruel while you've got the chance.'

The Possum wished to turn the matter off by saying, 'I see the price of eggs has gone up again', but Bill gave him a punch on the snout that bent it like a carrot, and Sam caught the Wombat such a flip with his flapper that he gave in at once.

'I shan't be able to fight any more this afternoon,' said the Wombat, 'as I've got sore feet.' The Possum

said hurriedly, 'We shall be late for that appointment', and they took their grindstone and off they went.

But when they were a safe distance away the Possum sang out: 'You'll repent this conduct. You'll repent bending a man's snout so that he can hardly see over it, let alone breathe through it with comfort', and the Wombat added, 'For shame, flapping a man with sore feet.'

'We laugh with scorn at threats,' said Bill, and he added as a warning –

> 'I don't repent a snout that's bent,
>   And if again I tap it,
> Oh, with a clout I'll bend that snout
>   With force enough to snap it.'

and Sam added for the Wombat's benefit –

> 'I take no shame to fight the lame
>   When they deserve to cop it.
> So do not try to pipe your eye,
>   Or with my flip I'll flop it.'

The puddin'-thieves disappeared over the hill and, as the evening happened to come down rather suddenly at that moment, Bill said, 'Business bein' over for the day, now's the time to set about makin' the camp fire.'

This was a welcome suggestion, for, as all travellers know, if you don't sit by a camp fire in the evening, you have to sit by nothing in the dark, which is a most unsociable way of spending your time. They found a comfortable nook under the hedge, where there were plenty of dry leaves to rest on, and there they built a fire, and put the billy on, and made tea. The tea and sugar and three tin cups and half a pound of mixed biscuits were brought out of the bag by Sam, while Bill cut slices of steak-and-kidney from the Puddin'. After that they had boiled jam-roll and apple-dumpling, as the fancy took them, for if you wanted a change of food from the Puddin', all you had to do was to whistle twice and turn the basin round.

After they had eaten as much as they wanted, the things were put away in the bag, and they settled down comfortably for the evening.

'This is what I call grand,' said Bill, cutting up his tobacco. 'Full-and-plenty to eat, pipes goin' and the evenin's enjoyment before us. Tune up on the mouth-organ, Sam, an' off she goes with a song.'

They had a mouth-organ in the bag which they took turns at playing, and Bill led off with a song which he said was called –

SPANISH GOLD

'When I was young I used to hold
    I'd run away to sea,
And be a Pirate brave and bold
    On the coast of Caribbee.

'For I sez to meself, "I'll fill me hold
With Spanish silver and Spanish gold,
And out of every ship I sink
I'll collar the best of food and drink.

'"For Caribbee, or Barbaree,
Or the shores of South Amerikee
Are all the same to a Pirate bold,
Whose thoughts are fixed on Spanish gold."

'So one fine day I runs away
    A Pirate for to be;
But I found there was never a Pirate left
    On the coast of Caribbee

'For Pirates go, but their next of kin
Are Merchant Captains, hard as sin,
And Merchant Mates as hard as nails
Aboard of every ship that sails.

'And I worked aloft and I worked below,
I worked wherever I had to go,
And the winds blew hard and the winds blew cold,
And I sez to meself as the ship she rolled,

'"O Caribbee! O Barbaree!
O shores of South Amerikee!
O, never go there: if the truth be told,
You'll get more kicks than Spanish gold."'

'And that's the truth, mate,' said Bill to Bunyip Bluegum. 'There ain't no pirates nowadays at sea, except
western ocean First Mates, and many's the bootin' I've
had for not takin' in the slack of the topsail halyards
fast enough to suit their fancy. It's a hard life, the sea,
and Sam here'll bear me out when I say that bein' hit
on the head with a belayin' pin while tryin' to pick up

the weather earing is an experience that no man wants twice. But toon up, and a song all round.'

'I shall sing you the "Penguin Bold",' said Sam, and, striking a graceful attitude, he sang this song –

'To see the penguin out at sea,
    And watch how he behaves,
Would prove that penguins cannot be
    And never shall be slaves.
You haven't got a notion
How penguins brave the ocean
    And laugh with scorn at waves.

'To see the penguin at his ease
    Performing fearful larks
With stingarees of all degrees,
    As well as whales and sharks;
The sight would quickly let you know
The great contempt that penguins show
    For stingarees and sharks.

32

'O see the penguin as he goes
  A-turning Catherine wheels,
Without repose upon the nose
  Of walruses and seals.
But bless your heart, a penguin feels
Supreme contempt for foolish seals,
  While he never fails, where'er he goes,
  To turn back-flaps on a walrus nose.'

'It's all very fine,' said the Puddin' gloomily, 'singing about the joys of being penguins and pirates, but how'd you like to be a Puddin' and be eaten all day long?'

And in a very gruff voice he sang as follows: –

'O, who would be a puddin',
 A puddin' in a pot,
A puddin' which is stood on
 A fire which is hot?
O sad indeed the lot
Of puddin's in a pot.

'I wouldn't be a puddin'
 If I could be a bird,
If I could be a wooden
 Doll, I would'n say a word.
Yes, I have often heard
It's grand to be a bird.

'But as I am a puddin',
 A puddin' in a pot,
I hope you get the stomach ache
 For eatin' me a lot.
I hope you get it hot,
You puddin'-eatin' lot!'

'Very well sung, Albert,' said Bill encouragingly, 'though you're a trifle husky in your undertones, which is no doubt due to the gravy in your innards. However, as a reward for bein' a bright little feller we shall have a slice of you all round before turnin' in for the night.'

So they whistled up the plum-duff side of the Puddin', and had supper. When that was done, Bill stood up and made a speech to Bunyip Bluegum.

'I am now about to put before you an important proposal,' said Bill. 'Here you are, a young intelligent feller, goin' about seein' the world by yourself. Here is

Sam an' me, two as fine fellers as ever walked, goin' about the world with a Puddin'. My proposal to you is – Join us, and become a member of the Noble Society of Puddin'-owners. The duties of the Society,' went on Bill, 'are light. The members are required to wander along the roads, indulgin' in conversation, song and story, eatin' at regular intervals at the Puddin'. And now, what's your answer?'

'My answer,' said Bunyip Bluegum, 'is, Done with you.' And, shaking hands warmly all round, they loudly sang –

THE PUDDIN'-OWNERS' ANTHEM

'The solemn word is plighted,
  The solemn tale is told,
We swear to stand united,
  Three puddin'-owners bold.

'When we with rage assemble,
  Let puddin'-snatchers groan;
Let puddin'-burglars tremble,
  They'll ne'er our puddin' own.

'Hurrah for puddin'-owning,
  Hurrah for Friendship's hand,
The puddin'-thieves are groaning
  To see our noble band.

'Hurrah, we'll stick together,
  And always bear in mind
To eat our puddin' gallantly,
  Whenever we're inclined.'

Having given three rousing cheers, they shook hands once more and turned in for the night. After such a busy day, walking, talking, fighting, singing, and eating puddin', they were all asleep in a pig's whisper.

Second Slice

THE Society of Puddin'-owners were up bright and early next morning, and had the billy on and tea made before six o'clock, which is the best part of the day, because the world has just had his face washed, and the air smells like Pears' soap.

'Aha,' said Bill Barnacle, cutting up slices of the Puddin', 'this is what I call grand. Here we are, after a splendid night's sleep on dry leaves, havin' a smokin' hot slice of steak-and-kidney for breakfast round the camp fire. What could be more delightful?'

'What indeed?' said Bunyip Bluegum sipping tea.

'Why, as I always say,' said Bill, 'if there's one thing more entrancin' than sittin' round a camp fire in the evenin' it's sitting round a camp fire in the mornin'. No bed and blankets and breakfast tables for Bill Barnacle. For as I says in my "Breakfast Ballad" –

> 'If there's anythin' better than lyin' on leaves,
>   It's risin' from leaves at dawnin',
> If there's anythin' better than sleepin' at eve,
>   It's wakin' up in the mawnin'.
>
> 'If there's anythin' better than camp firelight,
>   It's bright sunshine on wakin'.
> If there's anythin' better than puddin' at night,
>   It's puddin' when day is breakin'.
>
> 'If there's anythin' better than singin' away
>   While the stars are gaily shinin',
> Why, it's singin' a song at dawn of day,
>   On puddin' for breakfast dinin'.'

There was a hearty round of applause at this song, for as Bunyip Bluegum remarked, 'Singing at breakfast should certainly be more commonly indulged in, as it greatly tends to enliven what is on most occasions a somewhat dull proceeding.'

'One of the great advantages of being a professional Puddin'-owner,' said Sam Sawnoff, 'is that songs at breakfast are always encouraged. None of the ordinary breakfast rules, such as scowling while eating, and saying the porridge is as stiff as glue and the eggs are as tough as leather, are observed. Instead, songs, roars of laughter, and boisterous jests are the order of the day. For example, this sort of thing,' added Sam, doing a rapid back-flap and landing with a thump on Bill's head. As Bill was unprepared for this act of boisterous humour, his face was pushed into the Puddin' with great violence, and the gravy was splashed in his eye.

'What d'yer mean, playin' such bungfoodlin' tricks on a man at breakfast?' roared Bill.

'What d'yer mean,' shouted the Puddin', 'playing such foodbungling tricks on a Puddin' being breakfasted at?'

'Breakfast humour, Bill, merely breakfast humour,' said Sam hastily.

'Humour's humour,' shouted Bill, 'but puddin' in the whiskers is no joke.'

'Whiskers in the Puddin' is worse than puddin' in the whiskers,' shouted the Puddin', standing up in his basin.

'Observe the rules, Bill,' said Sam hurriedly. 'Boisterous humour at the breakfast table must be greeted with roars of laughter.'

'To Jeredelum with the rules,' shouted Bill. 'Pushing a man's face into his own breakfast is beyond rules or reason, and deserves a punch in the gizzard.'

Seeing matters arriving at this unpromising situation, Bunyip Bluegum interposed by saying, 'Rather than allow this happy occasion to be marred by unseemly recriminations, let us, while admitting that our admirable friend, Sam, may have unwittingly disturbed the composure of our admirable friend, Bill, at the expense of our admirable Puddin's gravy, let us, I say, by the simple act of extending the hand of friendship, dispel in an instant these gathering clouds of disruption. In the words of the poem –

> 'Then let the fist of Friendship
> Be kept for Friendship's foes.
> Ne'er let that hand in anger land
> On Friendship's holy nose.'

These fine sentiments at once dispelled Bill's anger. He shook hands warmly with Sam, wiped the gravy from his face, and resumed breakfast with every appearance of hearty good humour.

The meal over, the breakfast things were put away in the bag, Sam and Bill took Puddin' between them, and all set off along the road, enlivening the way with song and story. Bill regaled them with portions of the 'Ballad of the *Salt Junk Sarah*', which is one of those songs that go on for ever. Its great advantage, as Bill remarked, was that as it hadn't got an ending it didn't need a beginning, so you could start it anywhere.

'As for instance,' said Bill, and he roared out –

> 'Ho, aboard the *Salt Junk Sarah*,
> Rollin' home across the line,
> The Bo'sun collared the Captain's hat
> And threw it in the brine.
> Rollin' home, rollin' home,
> Rollin' home across the foam,
> The Captain sat without a hat
> The whole way rollin' home.'

Entertaining themselves in this way as they strolled along, they were presently arrested by shouts of 'Fire! Fire!' and a Fireman in a large helmet came bolting down the road, pulling a fire hose behind him.

'Aha!' said Bill. 'Now we shall have the awe-inspirin' spectacle of a fire to entertain us,' and, accosting the Fireman, he demanded to know where the fire was.

'The fact is,' said the Fireman, 'that owing to the size of this helmet I can't see where it is; but if you will kindly glance at the surrounding district, you'll see it about somewhere.'

They glanced about and, sure enough, there was a fire burning in the next field. It was only a cowshed, certainly, but it was blazing very nicely, and well worth looking at.

'Fire,' said Bill, 'in the form of a common cowshed, is burnin' about nor'-nor'-east as the crow flies.'

'In that case,' said the Fireman, 'I invite all present bravely to assist in putting it out. But,' he added impressively, 'if you'll take my advice, you'll shove that

Puddin' in this hollow log and roll a stone agen the end to keep him in, for if he gets too near the flames he'll be cooked again and have his flavour ruined.'

'This is a very sensible feller,' said Bill, and though Puddin' objected strongly, he was at once pushed into a log and securely fastened in with a large stone.

'How'd you like to be shoved in a blooming log,' he shouted at Bill, 'when you was burning with anxiety to see the fire?' but Bill said severely, 'Be sensible, Albert, fires is too dangerous to Puddin's flavours.'

No more time was lost in seizing the hose and they set off with the greatest enthusiasm. For, as everyone knows, running with the reel is one of the grand joys of being a fireman. They had the hose fixed to a garden tap in no time, and soon were all hard at work, putting out the fire.

Of course there was a great deal of smoke and shouting, and getting tripped up by the hose, and it was by the merest chance Bunyip Bluegum glanced back in time to see the Wombat in the act of stealing the Puddin' from the hollow log.

'Treachery is at work,' he shouted.

'Treachery,' roared Bill, and with one blow on the snout knocked the Fireman endways on into the burning cinders, where his helmet fell off, and exposed the countenance of that snooting, snouting scoundrel, the Possum.

The Possum, of course, hadn't expected to have his disguise pierced so swiftly, and, though he managed to scramble out of the fire in time to save his bacon, he was considerably singed down the back.

'What a murderous attack!' he exclaimed. 'O, what a brutal attempt to burn a man alive!' and as some hot cinders had got down his back he gave a sharp yell and ran off, singeing and smoking. Bill, distracted with rage, ran after the Possum, then changed his mind and ran after the Wombat, so that, what with running first after one and then after the other, they both had time to get clean away, and disappeared over the skyline.

'I see it all,' shouted Bill, casting himself down in despair. 'Them low puddin'-thieves has borrowed a fireman's helmet, collared a hose, an' set fire to a cowshed in order to lure us away from the Puddin'.'

'The whole thing's a low put-up job on our noble credulity,' said Sam, casting himself down beside Bill.

'It's one of the most frightful things that's ever happened,' said Bill.

'It's worse than treading on tacks with bare feet,' said Sam.

'It's worse than bein' caught stealin' fowls,' said Bill.

'It's worse than bein' stood on by cows,' said Sam.

'It's almost as bad as havin' an uncle called Aldobrantifoscofornio,' said Bill, and they both sang loudly –

'It's worse than weevils, worse than warts,
　It's worse than corns to bear.
It's worse than havin' several quarts
　Of treacle in your hair.

'It's worse than beetles in the soup,
　It's worse than crows to eat.
It's worse than wearin' small-sized boots
　Upon your large-sized feet.

'It's worse than kerosene to boose,
　It's worse than ginger hair.
It's worse than anythin' to lose
　A Puddin' rich and rare.'

Bunyip Bluegum reproved this despondency, saying, 'Come, come, this is no time for giving way to despair. Let us, rather, by the fortitude of our bearing prove ourselves superior to this misfortune and, with the energy of justly enraged men, pursue these malefactors, who have so richly deserved our vengeance. Arise!'

'Bravely spoken,' said Bill, immediately recovering from despair.

> 'The grass is green, the day is fair,
>   The dandelions abound.
> Is this a time for sad despair
>   And sitting on the ground?
>
> 'Our Puddin' in some darksome lair
>   In iron chains is bound,
> While puddin'-snatchers on him fare,
>   And eat him by the pound.

'Let gloom give way to angry glare,
  Let weak despair be drowned,
Let vengeance in its rage declare
  Our Puddin' must be found.

'Then let's resolve to do and dare.
  Let teeth with rage be ground.
Let voices to the heavens declare
  Our Puddin' MUST be found.'

'Those gallant words have fired our blood,' said Sam, and they both shook hands with Bunyip, to show that they were now prepared to follow the call of vengeance.

'In order to investigate this dastardly outrage,' said Bunyip, 'we must become detectives, and find a clue. We must find somebody who has seen a singed possum. Once traced to their lair, mother-wit will suggest some means of rescuing our Puddin'.'

They set off at once, and, after a brisk walk, came to a small house with a signboard on it saying, 'Henderson Hedgehog, Horticulturist'. Henderson himself was in the garden, horticulturing a cabbage, and they asked him if he had chanced to see a singed possum that morning.

'What's that? What, what?' said Henderson Hedgehog, and when they had repeated the question, he said, 'You must speak up, I'm a trifle deaf.'

'Have you seen a singed possum?' shouted Bill.

'I can't hear you,' said Henderson.

'Have you seen a SINGED POSSUM?' roared Bill.

'To be sure,' said Henderson, 'but the turnips are backward.'

'Turnips be stewed,' yelled Bill in such a tremendous voice that he blew his own hat off. 'HAVE YOU SEEN A SINGED POSSUM?'

'Good season for wattle blossom,' said Henderson. 'Well, yes, but a very poor season for carrots.'

'A man might as well talk to a carrot as try an' get sense out of this runt of a feller,' said Bill, disgusted. 'Come an' see if we can't find someone that it won't bust a man's vocal cords gettin' information out of.'

They left Henderson to his horticulturing and walked on till they met a Parrot who was a Swagman, or a Swagman who was a Parrot. He must have been one or the other, if not both, for he had a bag and a swag, and a beak, and a billy, and a thundering bad temper into the bargain, for the moment Bill asked him if he had met a singed possum he shouted back –

'Me eat a singed possum! I wouldn't eat a possum if he was singed, roasted, boiled, or fried.'

'Not ett – met,' shouted Bill. 'I said, met a singed possum.'

'Why can't yer speak plainly, then,' said the Parrot. 'Have you got a fill of tobacco on yer?'

He took out his pipe and scowled at Bill.

'Here you are,' said Bill. 'Cut a fill an' answer the question.'

'All in good time,' said the Parrot, and he added to Sam, 'You got any tobacco?'

Sam handed him a fill, and he put it in his pocket. 'You ain't got any tobacco,' he said scornfully to Bunyip Bluegum. 'I can see that at a glance. You're one of the non-smoking sort, all fur and feathers.'

'Here,' said Bill angrily. 'Enough o' this beatin' about the bush. Answer the question.'

'Don't be impatient,' said the Parrot. 'Have you got a bit o' tea an' sugar on yer?'

'Here's yer tea an' sugar,' said Bill, handing a little of each out of the bag. 'And that's the last thing you get. Now will you answer the question?'

'Wot question?' asked the Parrot.

'Have yer seen a singed possum?' roared Bill.

'No, I haven't,' said the Parrot, and he actually had the insolence to laugh in Bill's face.

'Of all the swivel-eyed, up-jumped, cross-grained, sons of a cock-eyed tinker,' exclaimed Bill, boiling with rage. 'If punching parrots on the beak wasn't too painful for pleasure, I'd land you a sockdolager on the muzzle that 'ud lay you out till Christmas. Come on, mates,' he added, 'it's no use wastin' time over this low-down, hook-nosed tobacco-grabber.' And leaving the evil-minded Parrot to pursue his evil-minded way, they hurried off in search of information.

The next person they spied was a Bandicoot carrying a watermelon. At a first glance you would have thought it was merely a watermelon walking by itself, but a second glance would have shown you that the walking was being done by a small pair of legs attached to the watermelon, and a third glance would have disclosed that the legs were attached to a Bandicoot.

They shouted, 'Hi, you with the melon!' to attract his attention, and set off running after him, and the Bandicoot, being naturally of a terrified disposition, ran for all he was worth. He wasn't worth much as a

runner, owing to the weight of the watermelon, and they caught him up half-way across the field.

Conceiving that his hour had come, the Bandicoot gave a shrill squeak of terror and fell on his knees.

'Take me watermelon,' he gasped, 'but spare me life.'

'Stuff an' nonsense,' said Bill. 'We don't want your life. What we want is some information. Have you seen a singed possum about this morning?'

'Singed possums, sir, yes sir, certainly sir,' gasped the Bandicoot, trembling violently.

'What!' exclaimed Bill, 'do yer mean to say you have seen a singed possum?'

'Singed possums, sir, yes sir,' gulped the Bandicoot. 'Very plentiful, sir, this time of the year, sir, owing to the bush fires, sir.'

'Rubbish,' roared Bill. 'I don't believe he's seen a singed possum at all.'

'No, sir,' quavered the Bandicoot. 'Certainly not, sir. Wouldn't think of seeing singed possums if there was any objection, sir.'

'You're a poltroon,' shouted Bill. 'You're a slaverin', quaverin', melon-carryin' nincompoop. There's no more chance of getting information out of you than out of a terrified Turnip.'

Leaving the Bandicoot to pursue his quavering, melon-humping existence, they set off again, Bill giving way to some very despondent expressions.

'As far as I can see,' he said, 'if we can't find somethin' better than stone-deaf hedgehogs, peevish parrots, and funkin' bandicoots we may as well give way to despair.'

Bunyip Bluegum was forced to exert his finest oratory to inspire them to another frame of mind. 'Let it never be said,' he exclaimed, 'that the unconquerable hearts of Puddin'-owners quailed before a parrot, a hedgehog, or a bandicoot.'

> 'Let hedgehogs deaf go delve and dig,
>   Immune from loudest howl,
> Let bandicoots lump melons big,
>   Let peevish parrots prowl.

> 'Shall puddin'-owners bow the head
>   At such affronts as these?
> No, No! March on, by anger led,
>   Our Puddin' to release.

> 'Let courage high resolve inflame
>   Our captive Pud to free;
> Our banner wave, our words proclaim
>   We march to victory!'

'Bravely sung,' exclaimed Bill, grasping Bunyip Bluegum by the hand, and they proceeded with expressions of the greatest courage and determination.

As a reward for this renewed activity, they got some useful information from a Rooster who was standing at his front gate looking up and down the road, and wishing to heaven that somebody would come along for him to talk to. They got, in fact, a good deal more information than they asked for, for the Rooster was one of those fine up-standing, bumptious skites who love to talk all day, in the heartiest manner, to total strangers while their wives do the washing.

'Singed possum,' he exclaimed, when they had put the usual question to him. 'Now, what an extraordinary thing that you should come along and ask me that question. What an astounding and incredible thing

that you should actually use the word "singed" in connexion with the word "possum". Though mind you, the word I had in my mind was not "singed", but "burning". And not "possum", but "feathers". Now, I'll tell you why. Only this morning, as I was standing here, I said to myself "somebody's been burning feathers". I called out at once to the wife – fine woman, the wife, you'll meet her presently – "Have you been burning feathers?" "No", says she. "Well," said I, "if you haven't been burning feathers, somebody else has." At the very moment that I'm repeating the words "feathers" and "burning" you come along and repeat the words "singed" and "possum". Instantly I call to mind that at the identical moment that I smelt something burning, I saw a possum passing this very gate, though whether he happened to be singed or not I didn't inquire.'

'Which way did he go?' inquired Bill excitedly.

'Now, let me see,' said the Rooster. 'He went down the road, turned to the right, gave a jump and a howl, and set off in the direction of Watkin Wombat's summer residence.'

'The very man we're after,' shouted Bill, and bolted off down the road, followed by the others, without taking any notice of the Rooster's request to wait a minute and be introduced to the wife.

'His wife may be all right,' said Bill as they ran, 'but what I say is, blow meetin' a bloomin' old Rooster's wife when you haven't got a year to waste listenin' to a bloomin' old Rooster.'

They followed the Rooster's directions with the utmost rapidity, and came to a large hollow tree with a door in the side and a notice-board nailed up which said, 'Watkin Wombat, Esq., Summer Residence'.

The door was locked, but it was clear that the puddin'-thieves were inside, because they heard the Possum say peevishly, 'You're eating too much, and here's me, most severely singed, not getting sufficient', and the Wombat was heard to say, 'What you want is soap', but the Possum said angrily, 'What I need is immense quantities of puddin'.'

The avengers drew aside to hold a consultation.

'What's to be done?' said Bill. 'It's no use knockin', because they'd look through the keyhole and refuse to come out, and, not bein' burglars, we can't bust the door in. It seems to me that there's nothin' for it but to give way to despair.'

'Never give way to despair while whiskers can be made from dry grass,' said Bunyip Bluegum, and suiting the action to the word, he swiftly made a pair of fine moustaches out of dried grass and stuck them on with wattle gum. 'Now, lend me your hat,' he said to Bill, and taking the hat he turned up the brim, dented in the top, and put it on. 'The bag is also required,' he said to Sam, and taking that in his hand and turning his coat inside out, he stood before them completely disguised.

'You two,' he said, 'must remain in hiding behind

the tree. You will hear me knock, accost the ruffians and hold them in conversation. The moment you hear me exclaim loudly, "Hey, Presto! Pots and Pans", you will dart out and engage the villains at fisticuffs. The rest leave to me.'

Waiting till the others were hidden behind the tree,

Bunyip rapped smartly on the door which opened presently and the Wombat put his head out cautiously.

'Have I the extreme pleasure of addressing Watkin Wombat, Esq.?' inquired Bunyip Bluegum, with a bow.

Of course, seeing a perfect stranger at the door, the Wombat had no suspicions, and said at once, 'Such is the name of him you see before you.'

'I have called to see you,' said Bunyip, 'on a matter of business. The commodity which I vend is Pootles's Patent Pudding Enlarger, samples of which I have in the bag. As a guarantee of good faith we are giving samples of our famous Enlarger away to all well-known Puddin'-owners. The Enlarger, one of the wonders of modern science, has but to be poured over the puddin', with certain necessary incantations, and the puddin' will be instantly enlarged to double its normal size.' He took some sugar from the bag and held it up. 'I am now about to hand you some of this wonderful discovery. But,' he added impressively, 'the operation of enlarging the puddin' is a delicate one, and must be performed in the open air. Produce your puddin', and I will at once apply Pootles's Patent with marvellous effect.'

'Of course it's understood that no charge is to be made,' said the Possum, hurrying out.

'No charge whatever,' said Bunyip Bluegum.

So on the principle of always getting something for nothing, as the Wombat said, Puddin' was brought out and placed on the ground.

'Now watch me closely,' said Bunyip Bluegum. He sprinkled the Puddin' with sugar, made several passes with his hands, and pronounced these words –

> 'Who incantations utters
> He generally mutters
>   His gruesome blasts and bans
> But I, you need not doubt it,
> Prefer aloud to shout it,
>   Hey, Presto! Pots and Pans.'

Out sprang Bill and Sam and set about the puddin'-thieves like a pair of windmills, giving them such a clip-clap clouting and a flip-flap flouting, that what with being punched and pounded, and clipped and clapped, they had only enough breath left to give two shrieks of despair while scrambling back into Watkin Wombat's Summer Residence, and banging the door behind them. The three friends had Puddin' secured in no time, and shook hands all round, congratulating Bunyip Bluegum on the success of his plan.

'Your noble actin',' said Bill, 'has saved our Puddin's life.'

'Them puddin'-thieves,' said Sam, 'was children in your hands.'

'We hear you,' sang out the Possum, and the Wombat added, 'Oh, what deceit!'

'Enough of you two,' shouted Bill. 'If we catch you sneakin' after our Puddin' again, you'll get such a beltin' that you'll wish you was vegetarians. And now,' said he, 'for a glorious reunion round the camp fire.'

And a glorious reunion they had, tucking into hot steak-and-kidney puddin' and boiled jam roll, which, after the exertions of the day, went down, as Bill said, 'Grand'.

'If them puddin'-thieves ain't sufferin' the agonies of despair at this very moment, I'll eat my hat along with the Puddin',' said Bill, exultantly.

'Indeed,' said Bunyip Bluegum, 'the consciousness that our enemies are deservedly the victims of acute mental and physical anguish, imparts, it must be admitted, an additional flavour to the admirable Puddin'.'

'Well spoken,' said Bill, admiringly. 'Which I will say, that for turning off a few well-chosen words no parson in the land is the equal of yourself.'

'Your health!' said Bunyip Bluegum.

The singing that evening was particularly loud and prolonged, owing to the satisfaction they all felt at the recovery of their beloved Puddin'. The Puddin', who had got the sulks over Sam's remarks that fifteen goes of steak-and-kidney were enough for any self-respecting man, protested against the singing, which, he said, disturbed his gravy. '"More eating and less noise" is my motto,' he said, and he called Bill a leather-headed old barrel organ for reproving him.

'Albert is a spoilt child, I fear,' said Bill, shoving him into the bag to keep him quiet, and without more ado, led off with –

> 'Ho! aboard the *Salt Junk Sarah*,
> Rollin' home around the Horn,
> The Bo'sun pulls the Captain's nose
> For treatin' him with scorn.

> 'Rollin' home, rollin' home,
> Rollin' home across the foam.
> The Bo'sun goes with thumps and blows
> The whole way rollin' home.'

'But,' said Bill to Bunyip Bluegum, after about fifteen verses of the *Salt Junk Sarah*, 'the superior skill, ingenuity and darin' with which you bested them puddin'-snatchers reminds me of a similar incident in Sam's youth, which I will now sing you. The incident, though similar as regards courage an' darin', is totally different in regard to everythin' else, and is entitled–

THE PENGUIN'S BRIDE

"'Twas on the *Saucy Soup Tureen*,
    That Sam was foremast hand,
When on the quarter-deck was seen
A maiding fit to be a Queen
    With her old Uncle stand.

'And Sam at once was sunk all
    In passion deep and grand,
But this here aged Uncle
He was the Hearl of Buncle
    And Sam a foremast hand.

'And Sam he chewed salt junk all
    Day with grief forlorn,
Because the Hearl of Buncle,
The lovely maiding's Uncle,
    Regarded him with scorn.

'When sailin' by Barbado,
    The *Saucy Soup Tureen*,
Before she could be stayed-O
Went down in a tornado,
    And never more was seen.

65

'The passengers were sunk all
    Beneath the ragin' wave,
The maiding and her Uncle,
The Noble Hearl of Buncle,
    Were saved by Sam the Brave.

'He saved the Noble Buncle
  By divin' off the poop.
The maiding in a funk all
He saved along with Uncle
  Upon a chicken coop.

'And this here niece of Buncle,
  When they got safe to land,
For havin' saved her Uncle,
The Noble Hearl of Buncle,
  She offered Sam her hand.

'And that old Uncle Buncle,
  For joy of his release,
On Burgundy got drunk all
Day in Castle Buncle,
  Which hastened his decease.

'The lovely maiding Buncle
  Inherited the land;
And, now her aged Uncle
Has gone, the Hearl of Buncle
  Is Sam, the foremast hand.'

'Of course,' said Sam modestly, 'the song goes too far in sayin' as how I married the Hearl's niece, because, for one thing, I ain't a marryin' man, and for another thing, what she really sez to me when we got to land was, "You're a noble feller, an' here's five shillin's for you, and any time you happen to be round our way, just give a ring at the servants' bell, and there'll always be a feed waitin' for you in the kitchen." However, you've got to have songs to fill in the time with, and when a feller's got a rotten word like Buncle to find rhymes for, there's no sayin' how a song'll end.'

'The exigencies of rhyme,' said Bunyip Bluegum, 'may stand excused from a too strict insistence on verisimilitude, so that the general gaiety is thereby promoted. And now,' he added, 'before retiring to rest, let us all join in song,' and grasping each other's hands they loudly sang –

THE PUDDIN'-OWNERS' EVENSONG

'Let feeble feeders stoop
To plates of oyster soup.
　　Let pap engage
　　The gums of age
And appetites that droop;
　　We much prefer to chew
　　A Steak-and-kidney stew.

'Let yokels coarse appease
Their appetites with cheese.
　　Let women dream
　　Of cakes and cream,
We scorn fal-lals like these;
　　Our sterner sex extols
　　The joy of boiled jam rolls.

'We scorn digestive pills;
Give us the food that fills;
Who bravely stuff
Themselves with Duff,
May laugh at Doctor's bills.
For medicine, partake
Of kidney, stewed with steak.

'Then plight our faith anew
Three puddin'-owners true,
Who boldly claim
In Friendship's name
The noble Irish stoo,
Hurrah, Hurrah, Hurroo!'

Third Slice

'AFTER our experience of yesterday,' said Bill Barnacle as the company of Puddin'-owners set off along the road with their Puddin', 'we shall have to be particularly careful. For what with low puddin'-thieves disguising themselves as firemen, and low Wombats

sneakin' our Puddin' while we're helpin' to put out fires, not to speak of all the worry and bother of tryin' to get information out of parrots and bandicoots an' hedgehogs, why, it's enough to make a man suspect his own grandfather of bein' a puddin'-snatcher.'

'As for me,' said Sam Sawnoff, practising boxing attitudes as he walked along, 'I feel like laying out the first man we meet on the off-chance of his being a puddin'-thief.'

'Indeed,' observed Bunyip Bluegum, 'to have one's noblest feelings outraged by reposing a too great trust in unworthy people, is to end by regarding all humanity with an equal suspicion.'

'If you ask my opinion,' said the Puddin' cynically, 'them puddin'-thieves are too clever for you; and, what's more, they're better eaters than you. Why,' said the Puddin', sneering at Bill, 'I'll back one puddin'-thief to eat more in a given time than three Puddin'-owners put together.'

'These are very treacherous sentiments, Albert,' said Bill sternly. 'These are very ignoble and shameless words,' but the Puddin' merely laughed scornfully, and called Bill a bun-headed old beetle-crusher.

'Very well,' said Bill, enraged, 'we shall see if a low puddin'-thief is better than a noble Puddin'-owner. When you see the terrible suspicions I shall indulge in to-day you'll regret them words.'

To prove his words Bill insisted on closely inspecting everybody he met, in case they should be puddin'-thieves in disguise.

To start off with, they had an unpleasant scene with a Kookaburra, a low larrikin who resented the way that Bill examined him.

'Who are you starin' at, Poodle's Whiskers?' he asked.

'Never mind,' said Bill. 'I'm starin' at you for a good an' sufficient reason.'

'Are yer?' said the Kookaburra. 'Well, all I can say is that if yer don't take yer dial outer the road I'll bloomin' well take an' bounce a gibber off yer crust,' and he followed them for quite a long way, singing out insulting things such as, 'You with the wire whiskers,' and 'Get onter the bloke with the face fringe.'

Bill, of course, treated this conduct with silent contempt. It was his rule through life, he said, never to fight people with beaks.

The next encounter they had was with a Flying-fox who, though not so vulgar and rude as the Kookaburra, was equally enraged because, as Bill had suspicions that he was the Possum disguised, he insisted on measuring him to see if he was the same length.

'Nice goings on, indeed,' said the Flying-fox, while Bill was measuring him, 'if a man can't go about his business without being measured by total strangers. A nice thing, indeed, to happen to Finglebury Flying-fox, the well-known and respected fruit stealer.'

However, he was found to be six inches too short, so they let him go, and he hurried off, saying, 'I shall have the Law on you for this, measuring a man in a public place without being licensed as a tailor.'

The third disturbance due to Bill's suspicions occurred while Bunyip Bluegum was in a grocer's shop. They had run out of tea and sugar, and happening to pass through the town of Bungledoo took the opportunity of laying in a fresh supply. If Bunyip hadn't been in the shop, as was pointed out afterwards, the trouble wouldn't have occurred. The first he heard of it was a scream of 'Help, help, murder is being done!' and rushing out of the

shop, what was his amazement to see no less a person than his Uncle Wattleberry bounding and plunging about the road with Bill hanging on to his whiskers, and Sam hanging on to one leg.

'I've got him,' shouted Bill. 'Catch a hold of his other leg and give me a chance to get his whiskers off.'

'But why are you taking his whiskers off?' inquired Bunyip Bluegum.

'Because they're stuck on with glue,' shouted Bill. 'I saw it at a glance. It's Watkin Wombat, Esq., disguised as a company promoter.'

'Dear me,' said Bunyip, hurriedly, 'you are making a mistake. This is not a puddin'-thief, this is an Uncle.'

'A what?' exclaimed Bill, letting go the whiskers.

'An Uncle,' replied Bunyip Bluegum.

'An Uncle,' roared Uncle Wattleberry. 'An Uncle of

the highest integrity. You have most disgracefully and unmercifully pulled an Uncle's whiskers.'

'I can assure you,' said Bill, 'I pulled them under the delusion that you was a disguised Wombat.'

'That is no excuse, sir,' bellowed Uncle Wattleberry. 'No one but an unmitigated ruffian would pull an Uncle's whiskers.

'Who but the basest scoundrel, double-eyed,
  Would pluck an Uncle's whiskers in their pride,
  What baseness, then, doth such a man disclose
  Who'd raise a hand to pluck an Uncle's nose?'

'If I've gone too far,' said Bill, 'I apologize. If I'd known you was an Uncle I wouldn't have done it.'

'Apologies are totally inadequate,' shouted Uncle Wattleberry. 'Nothing short of felling you to the earth with an umbrella could possibly atone for the outrage. You are a danger to the whisker-growing public. You have knocked my hat off, pulled my whiskers, and tried to remove my nose.'

'Pullin' your nose,' said Bill, solemnly, 'is a mistake any man might make, for I put it to all present, as man to man, if that nose don't look as if it's only gummed on.'

All present were forced to admit that it was a mistake that any man might make. 'Any man,' as Sam remarked, 'would think he was doing you a kindness by trying to pull it off.'

'Allow me to point out also, my dear Uncle,' said Bunyip Bluegum, 'that your whiskers were responsible for this seeming outrage. Let your anger, then, be assuaged by the consciousness that you are the victim, not of malice, but of the misfortune of wearing whiskers.'

'How now,' exclaimed Uncle Wattleberry. 'My nephew Bunyip among these sacrilegious whisker-pluckers and nose-pullers. My nephew, not only aiding and abetting these ruffians, but seeking to palliate their crimes! This is too much. My feelings are such that nothing but bounding and plunging can relieve them.'

And thereupon did Uncle Wattleberry proceed to bound and plunge with the greatest activity, shouting all the while –

> 'You need not think I bound and plunge
> Like this in festive mood.
> I bound that bounding may expunge
> The thought of insult rude.

> 'An Uncle's rage must seek relief,
> His anger must be drowned;
> It is to soothe an Uncle's grief
> That thus I plunge and bound.

> 'I bound and plunge, I seethe with rage,
> My mighty anger seeks
> So much relief that I engage
> To plunge and bound for weeks.'

Seeing that there was no possibility of inducing Uncle Wattleberry to look at the affair in a reasonable light, they walked off and left him to continue his bounding and plunging for the amusement of the people of Bungledoo, who brought their chairs out on to the footpath in order to enjoy the sight at their ease. Bill's intention to regard everybody he met with suspicion was somewhat damped by this mistake, and he said there ought to be a law to prevent a man going about looking as if he was a disguised puddin'-thief.

The most annoying part of it all was that when the puddin'-thieves did make their appearance they weren't disguised at all. They were dressed as common ordinary

puddin'-thieves, save that the Possum carried a bran bag in his hand and the Wombat waved a white flag.

'Well, if this isn't too bad,' shouted Bill, enraged. 'What d'you mean, comin' along in this unexpected way without bein' disguised?'

'No, no,' sang out the Possum. 'No disguises to-day.'

'No fighting, either,' said the Wombat.

'No disguises, no fighting, and no puddin'-stealing,'

said the Possum. 'Nothing but the fairest and most honourable dealings.'

'If you ain't after our Puddin', what are you after?' demanded Bill.

'We're after bringing you a present in this bag,' said the Possum.

'Absurd,' said Bill. 'Puddin'-thieves don't give presents away.'

'Don't say that, Bill,' said the Possum, solemnly. 'If you only knew what noble intentions we have, you'd be ashamed of them words.'

'You'd blush to hear your voice a-utterin' of them,' said the Wombat.

'I can't make this out at all,' said Bill, scratching his head. 'The idea of a puddin'-thief offering a man a present dumbfounds me, as the saying goes.'

'No harm is intended,' said the Possum, and the Wombat added: 'Harm is as far from our thoughts as from the thoughts of angels.'

'Well, well,' said Bill, at length. 'I'll just glance at it first, to see what it's like.'

But the Possum shook his head. 'No, no, Bill,' he said, 'no glancing,' and the Wombat added: 'To prove that no deception is intended, all heads must look in the bag together.'

'What's to be done about this astoundin' predicament?' said Bill. 'If there is a present, of course we may as well have it. If there ain't a present, of course we shall simply have to punch their snouts as usual.'

'One must confess,' said Bunyip Bluegum, 'to the prompting of a certain curiosity as to the nature of this present'; and Sam added, 'Anyway, there's no harm in having a look at it.'

'No harm whatever,' said the Possum, and he held the bag open invitingly. The Puddin'-owners hesitated a moment, but the temptation was too strong, and they all looked in together. It was a fatal act. The Possum whipped the bag over their heads, the Wombat whipped a rope round the bag, and there they were, helpless.

The worst of it was that the Puddin', being too short to look in, was left outside, and the puddin'-thieves grabbed him at once and ran off like winking. To add to the Puddin'-owners' discomfiture there was a considerable amount of bran in the bag; and, as Bill said afterwards, 'if there's anything worse than losing a valuable Puddin', it's bran in the whiskers'. They bounded and plunged about, but soon had to stop that on account of treading on each other's toes – especially

Sam's, who endured agonies, having no boots on.

'What a frightful calamity,' groaned Bill giving way to despair.

'It's worse than being chased by natives on the Limpopo River,' said Sam.

'It's worse than fighting Arabs single-handed,' croaked Bill.

'It's almost as bad as being pecked on the head by eagles,' said Sam, and in despair they sang in muffled tones –

> 'O what a fearful fate it is,
>   O what a frightful fag,
> To have to walk about like this
>   All tied up in a bag.

> 'Our noble confidence has sent
>   Us on this fearful jag;
> In noble confidence we bent
>   To look inside this bag.

> 'Deprived of air, in dark despair
> Upon our way we drag;
> Condemned for evermore to wear
> This frightful, fearsome bag.'

Bunyip Bluegum reproved this faint-heartedness, saying, 'As our misfortunes are due to exhibiting too great a trust in scoundrels, so let us bear them with the greater fortitude. As in innocence we fell, so let our conduct in this hour of dire extremity be guided by the courageous endurance of men whose consciences are free from guilt.'

These fine words greatly stimulated the others, and they endured with fortitude, walking on Sam's feet for an hour and a half, when the sound of footsteps apprised them that a traveller was approaching.

This traveller was a grave, elderly dog named Benjimen Brandysnap, who was going to market with eggs. Seeing three people walking in a bag he naturally supposed they were practising for the sports, but on hearing their appeals for help he very kindly undid the rope.

'Preserver,' exclaimed Bill, grasping him by the hand.

'Noble being,' said Sam.

'Guardian angel of oppressed Puddin'-owners,' said Bunyip Bluegum.

Benjimen was quite overcome by these expressions of

esteem, and handed round eggs, which were eaten on the spot.

'And now,' said Bill, again shaking hands with their preserver, 'I am about to ask you a most important question. Have you seen any puddin'-thieves about this mornin'?'

'Puddin'-thieves,' said Benjimen. 'Let me see. Now that you mention it, I remember seeing two puddin'-thieves at nine-thirty this morning. But they weren't stealing puddin's. They were engaged stealing a bag out of my stable. I was busy at the time whistling to the carrots, or I'd have stopped them.'

'This is most important information,' said Bill. 'It proves this must be the very bag they stole. In what direction did the scoundrels go, friend, after stealing your bag?'

'As I was engaged at the moment feeding the parsnips, I didn't happen to notice,' said Benjimen. 'But at this season puddin'-thieves generally go south-east, owing to the price of onions.'

'In that case,' said Bill, 'we shall take a course north-west, for it's my belief that havin' stolen our Puddin' they'll make back to winter quarters.'

'We will pursue to the north-west with the utmost vigour,' said Bunyip.

'Swearin' never to give in till revenge has been inflicted and our Puddin' restored to us,' said Bill.

'In order to exacerbate our just anger,' said Bunyip Bluegum, 'let us sing as we go –

THE PUDDIN'-OWNERS' QUEST

'On a terrible quest we run north-west,
  In a terrible rage we run;
With never a rest we run north-west
  Till our terrible work is done.

Without delay
Away, away,
In a terrible rage we run all day.

'By our terrible zest you've doubtless guessed
That vengeance is our work;
For we seek the nest with terrible zest
Where the puddin'-snatchers lurk.
With rage, with gloom,
With fret and fume,
We seek the puddin'-snatchers' doom.'

They ran north-west for two hours without seeing a sign of the puddin'-thieves. Benjimen ran with them to exact revenge for the theft of his bag. It was hot work running, and having no Puddin' they couldn't have lunch, but Benjimen very generously handed eggs all round again.

'Eggs is all very well,' said Bill, eating them in despair, 'but they don't come up to Puddin' as a regular diet, and all I can say is, that if that Puddin' ain't restored soon I shall go mad with grief.'

'I shall go mad with rage,' said Sam, and they both sang loudly –

> 'Go mad with grief or mad with rage,
> It doesn't matter whether;
> Our Puddin's left this earthly stage,
> So in despair we must engage
> To both go mad together.'

'I have a suggestion to make,' said Bunyip Bluegum, 'which will at once restore your wonted good-humour. Observe me.'

He looked about till he found a piece of board, and wrote this notice on it with his fountain pen –

A GRAND PROCESSION OF
THE AMALGAMATED SOCIETY OF
PUDDINGS WILL PASS HERE
AT 2.30 TO-DAY

This he hung on a tree. 'Now,' said he, 'all that remains to be done is to hide behind this bush. The news of the procession will spread like wildfire through the district, and the puddin'-thieves, unable to resist such a spectacle, will come hurrying to view the procession. The rest will be simply a matter of springing out on them like lions.'

'Superbly reasoned,' said Bill, grasping Bunyip by the hand.

They all hid behind the bush and a crow, who happened to be passing, read the sign and flew off at once to spread the news through the district.

In fifteen minutes, by Bill's watch, the puddin'-thieves came running down the road, and took up a position on a stump to watch the procession. They had evidently been disturbed in the very act of eating

A Grand Procession of the Amalgamated Society of Puddings will pass here at 2.30 To day

A Grand Procession of
the Amalgamated Society of
Puddings will pass here
at 2·30 To day

Puddin', for the Possum was still masticating a mouthful; and the Wombat had stuck the Puddin' in his hat,
and put his hat on his head, which clearly proved him

to be a very ill-bred fellow, for in good society wearing puddin's on the head is hardly ever done.

Bill and Sam, who were like bloodhounds straining at the leash, sprang out and confronted the scoundrels, while Bunyip and Ben got behind in order to cut off their retreat.

'We've got you at last,' said Bill, sparring up at the Possum with the fiercest activity. 'Out with our Puddin', or prepare for a punch on the snout.'

The Possum turned pale and the Wombat hastily got behind him.

'Puddin',' said the Possum, acting amazement. 'What strange request is this?'

'What means this strange request?' asked the Wombat.

'No bungfoodlin',' said Bill sternly. 'Produce the Puddin' or prepare for death.'

'Before bringing accusations,' said the Possum, 'prove where the Puddin' is.'

'It's under that feller's hat,' roared Bill, pointing at the Wombat.

'Prove it,' said the Wombat.

'You can't wear hats that high, without there's puddin's under them,' said Bill.

'That's not puddin's,' said the Possum; 'that's ventilation. He wears his hat like that to keep his brain cool.'

'Very well,' said Bill. 'I call on Ben Brandysnap, as an independent witness whose bag has been stolen, to prove what's under that hat.'

Ben put on his spectacles in order to study the Wombat carefully, and gravely pronounced this judgement –

> 'When you see a hat
> Stuck up like that
>   You remark with some surprise,
> "Has he been to a shop,
> And bought for his top
>   A hat of the largest size?"

> 'Or else you say,
> As you note the way
>   He wears it like a wreath,
> "It cannot be fat
> That bulges his hat;
>   He's got something underneath."

> 'But whether or not
> It's a Puddin' he's got
>   Can only be settled by lifting his pot.
> Or by taking a stick,
> A stone or a brick,
>   And hitting him hard on the head with it quick.

> If he yells, you hit fat,
> If he doesn't, well that
>   Will prove it's a Puddin' that's under his hat.'

'Now are you satisfied?' asked Bill, and they all shouted –

> 'Hurrah! hurray!
>   Just listen to that;
> He knows the way
>   To bell the cat.
> You'd better obey
>   His judgement pat,

> 'Without delay
>   Remove the hat;
> It's tit-for-tat,
>   We tell you flat,
> You'll find it pay
>   To lift your hat.

> 'Obey the mandate of our chosen lawyer,
>   Remove that hat, or else we'll do it faw yer.'

'No, no,' said the Possum, shaking his head. 'No removing people's hats. Removing hats is larceny, and you'll get six months for it.'

'No bashing heads, either,' said the Wombat. 'That's manslaughter, and we'll have you hung for it.'

Bill scratched his head. 'This is an unforeseen predicament,' he said. 'Just mind them puddin'-thieves a minute, Ben, while we has a word in private.' He took Sam and Bunyip aside, and almost gave way to despair. 'What a frightful situation,' wailed he. 'We can't unlawfully take a puddin'-thief's hat off, and while it remains on who's to prove our Puddin's under it? This is one of the worst things that's happened to Sam and me for years.'

'It's worse than being chased by wart-hogs,' said Sam.

'It's worse than rolling off a cowshed,' said Bill.

'It's worse than wearing soup tureens for hats,' said Sam.

'It's almost as bad as swallowing thistle buttons,' said Bill, and both sang loudly –

> 'It's worse than running in a fright,
>   Pursued by Polar bears;
>   It's worse than being caught at night
>   By lions in their lairs.
>
> 'It's worse than barrel organs when
>   They play from night till morn;
>   It's worse than having large-sized men
>   A-standing on your corn.
>
> 'It's worse than when at midnight you
>   Tread on a silent cat,
>   To have a puddin'-snatcher who
>   Will not remove his hat.'

'All is not yet lost,' said Bunyip Bluegum. 'Without reverting to violent measures, I will engage to have the hat removed.'

'You will?' exclaimed Bill, grasping Bunyip by the hand.

'I will,' said Bunyip firmly. 'All I ask is that you strike a dignified attitude in the presence of these scoundrels, and, at a given word, follow my example.'

They all struck a dignified attitude in front of the puddin'-thieves, and Bunyip Bluegum, raising his hat, struck up the National Anthem, the others joining in with superb effect.

'Hats off in honour to our King,' shouted Bill, and off came all the hats. The puddin'-thieves, of course,

were helpless. The Wombat had to take his hat off, or prove himself disloyal, and there was Puddin' sitting on his head.

'Now who's a liar?' shouted Bill, hitting the Possum a swinging blow on the snout, while Sam gave the Wombat one of his famous over-arm flip flaps that knocked all the wind out of him. The Wombat tried to escape punishment by shouting, 'Never strike a man with a Puddin' on his head'; but, now that their guilt was proved, Bill and Sam were utterly remorseless, and gave the puddin'-thieves such a trouncing that their shrieks pierced the firmament. When this had been done, all hands gave them an extra thumping in the interests of common morality. Eggs were rubbed in their hair by Benjimen, and Bill and Sam attended to the beating and snout-bending, while Bunyip did the reciting. Standing on a stump, he declaimed –

'The blows you feel we do not deal
  In common, vulgar thumping;
To higher motives we appeal –
It is to teach you not to steal,
  Your head we now are bumping.
  You need not go on pumping
Appeals for kinder dealing,
  We like to watch you jumping,
We like to hear you squealing.
  We rather think this thumping
Will take a bit of healing.

We hope these blows upon the nose,
These bended snouts, these tramped-on toes,
These pains that you are feeling
The truth will be revealing
How wrong is puddin'-stealing.'

Then, with great solemnity, he recited the following fine moral lesson –

'A puddin'-thief, as I've heard tell,
Quite lost to noble feeling,
Spent all his days, and nights as well,
In constant puddin'-stealing.

'He stole them here, he stole them there,
He knew no moderation;
He stole the coarse, he stole the rare,
He stole without cessation.

'He stole the steak-and-kidney stew
  That housewives in a rage hid;
He stole the infant's Puddin' too,
  The Puddin' of the aged.

'He lived that Puddin's he might lure,
  Into his clutches stealthy;
He stole the Puddin' of the poor,
  The Puddin' of the wealthy.

'This evil wight went forth one night
  Intent on puddin'-stealing,
When he beheld a hidden light
  A secret room revealing.

'Within he saw a fearful man,
  With eyes like coals a-glowing,
Whose frightful whiskers over-ran
  His face, like weeds a-blowing;

'And there this fearful, frightful man,
  A sight to set you quaking,
With pot and pan and curse and ban,
  Began a Puddin' making.

'"Twas made of buns and boiling oil,
    A carrot and some nails-O!
A lobster's claws, the knobs off doors,
    An onion and some snails-O!

'A pound of fat, an old man rat,
    A pint of kerosene-O!
A box of tacks, some cobbler's wax,
    Some gum and glycerine-O!

'Gunpowder too, a hob-nailed shoe,
    He stirred into his pottage;
Some Irish stew, a pound of glue,
    A high explosive sausage.

'The deed was done, that frightful one,
    With glare of vulture famished,
Blew out the light, and in the night
    Gave several howls, and vanished.

'Our thieving lout, ensconced without,
    Came through the window slinking;
He grabbed the pot and on the spot
    Began to eat like winking.

'He ate the lot, this guzzling sot –
    Such appetite amazes –
Until those high explosives wrought
Within his tum a loud report,
    And blew him all to blazes.

'For him who steals ill-gotten meals
    Our moral is a good un.
We hope he feels that it reveals
    The danger he is stood in
Who steals a high explosive bomb,
    Mistaking it for Puddin'.'

The puddin'-thieves wept loudly while this severe rebuke was being administered, and promised, with sobs, to amend their evil courses, and in the future to abstain from unlawful puddin'-snatching.

'Your words,' said the Possum, 'has pierced our brains with horror and remorse'; and the Wombat added: 'From this time onwards our thoughts will be as far removed from Puddin' as is the thoughts of angels.'

'We have heard that before,' said Bunyip Bluegum; 'but let us hope that this time your repentance is sincere. Let us hope that the tenderness of your snouts will be, if I may be permitted a flight of poetic fancy, a guiding star to lure your steps along the path of virtue –

> 'For he who finds his evil course is ended
> By having of his snout severely bended,
> Along that path of virtue may be sent
> Where virtuous snouts are seldom ever bent.'

With that the puddin'-thieves went over the hill, the sun went down and evening arrived, punctual to the minute.

'Ah,' said Bill. 'It's a very fortunate thing that evenin's come along at this time, for, if it hadn't, we couldn't have waited dinner any longer. But, before preparin' for a night of gaiety, dance, and song, I have a proposal to put before my feller Puddin'-owners. I propose to invite our friend Ben here to join us round the camp fire. He has proved himself a very decent feller, free with his eggs, and as full of revenge against puddin'-thieves as ourselves.'

'Hospitably spoken,' said Bunyip Bluegum, and the Puddin'-owners sang –

> 'Come join us we intreat,
>   Come join us we implore,
>   In Friendship's name our guest we claim,
>   And Friendship's name is law.
>
> 'We've Puddin' here a treat,
>   We've Puddin' here galore;
>   Do not decline to stay and dine,
>   Our Puddin' you'll adore.
>
> 'Our Puddin', we repeat,
>   You really cannot beat,
>   And here are we its owners three
>   Who graciously intreat
>   You'll be at our request,
>   The Puddin'-owners' guest.'

'For these sentiments of esteem, admiration, and respect,' said Ben, 'I thank you. As one market-gardener to three Puddin'-owners, I may say I wouldn't wish to eat the Puddin' of three finer fellers than yourselves.'

With this cordial understanding they set about preparing the camp fire, and the heartiest expressions of friendship were indulged in while the Puddin' was being passed round. As Bunyip aptly remarked –

> 'All Fortune's buffets he can surely pardon her,
> Who claims as guest our courteous Market Gardener.'

To which Benjimen handsomely replied –

> 'Still happier he, who meets three Puddin'-owners,
> Whose Puddin' is the equal of its donors.'

And, indeed, a very pleasant evening they had round the camp fire.

Fourth Slice

'This is what I call satisfactory,' said Bill, as they sat at breakfast next morning. 'It's a great relief to the mind to know that them puddin'-thieves is sufferin' the agonies of remorse, and that our Puddin' is safe from bein' stolen every ten minutes.'

'You're a bun-headed old optimist,' said the Puddin' rudely. 'Puddin'-thieves never suffer from remorse. They only suffer from blighted hopes and suppressed activity.'

'Have you no trust in human nature, Albert?' asked Bill, sternly. 'Don't you know that nothin' gives a man greater remorse than havin' his face punched, his toes trod on, and eggs rubbed in his hair?'

'I have grave doubts myself,' said Bunyip Bluegum, 'as to the sincerity of their repentance'; and Ben Brandysnap said that, speaking as a market gardener, his experience of carrot catchers, onion snatchers, pumpkin pouncers, and cabbage grabbers induced him to hold the opinion that shooting them with pea-rifles was the only sure way to make them feel remorse.

In fact, as Sam said –

> 'The howls and groans of pain and grief,
>   The accents of remorse,
>   Extracted from a puddin'-thief
>   Are all put on, of course.'

'Then, all I can say is,' cried Bill, enraged, 'if there's any more of this business of puddin'-thieves, disguised as firemen, stealing our Puddin', and puddin'-thieves, not disguised at all, shovin' bags over our heads, blow me if I don't give up Puddin'-owning in despair and take to keepin' carrots for a livin'.'

The Puddin' was so furious at this remark that they were forced to eat an extra slice all round to pacify him, in spite of which he called Bill a turnip-headed old carrot-cruncher, and other insulting names. However, at length they set out on the road, Bill continuing to air some very despondent remarks.

'For what is the good of havin' a noble trustin' nature,' said he, 'for every low puddin'-thief in the land to take advantage of? As far as I can see, the only thing to do is to punch every snout we meet, and chance the odds it belongs to a puddin'-thief.'

'Come,' said Bunyip Bluegum, 'I see you are not your wonted, good-humoured self this morning. As a means of promoting the general gaiety, I call on you to sing the *Salt Junk Sarah* without delay.'

This was immediately effective, and Bill with the greatest heartiness roared out –

> 'Ho, aboard the *Salt Junk Sarah*
> Rollin' round the ocean wide,
> The bo'sun's mate, I grieve to state,
> He kissed the bo'sun's bride.

'Rollin' home, rollin' home,
Home across the foam;
The bo'sun rose and punched his nose
And banged him on the dome.'

At about the fifteenth verse they came to the town of Tooraloo, and that put a stop to the singing, because you can't sing in the public streets unless you are a musician or a nuisance. The town of Tooraloo is one of those dozing, snoozing, sausage-shaped places where all the people who aren't asleep are only half awake, and where dogs pass away their lives on the footpaths, and you fall over cows when taking your evening stroll.

There was a surprise awaiting them at Tooraloo, for the moment they arrived two persons in bell-toppers and long-tailed coats ran out from behind a fence and fell flat on their backs in the middle of the road, yelling 'Help, help! thieves and ruffians are at work!'

The travellers naturally stared with amazement at

this peculiar conduct. The moment the persons in bell-toppers caught sight of them they sprang up, and striking an attitude expressive of horror, shouted:

'Behold the puddin'-thieves!'

'Behold the what?' exclaimed Bill.

'Puddin'-thieves,' said one of the bell-topperers. 'For well you know that that dear Puddin' in your hand has been stolen from its parents and guardians, which is ourselves.' And the other bell-topperer added, 'Deny it not, for with that dear Puddin' in your hand your guilt is manifest.'

'Well, if this ain't enough to dumbfound a codfish,' exclaimed Bill. 'Here's two total strangers, disguised as undertakers, actually accusin' us of stealin' our own Puddin'. Why, it's outside the bounds of comprehension!'

'It's enough to stagger the senses,' said Sam.

'It's enough to daze the mind with horror,' said Bill.

'Come, come,' said the bell-toppers, 'cease these expressions of amazement and hand over the stolen Puddin'.'

'What d'yer mean,' exclaimed Bill, 'by calling this a stolen Puddin'? It's a respectable steak-and-kidney, apple-dumplin', grand digestive Puddin', and any fellers in pot-hats sayin' it's a stolen Puddin' is scoundrels of the deepest dye.'

'Never use such words to people wearing bell-toppers,' said one of the bell-toppers, and the other added, 'With that dear Puddin' gazing up to heaven, how can you use such words?'

'All very fine, no doubt,' sneered Bill, 'but if you ain't scoundrels of the deepest dye, remove them hats and prove you ain't afraid to look us in the eye.'

'No, no,' said the first bell-topper. 'No removing hats at present on account of sunstroke, and colds in the head, and doctor's orders. My doctor said to me only this morning, "Never remove your hat." Those were his words. "Let it be your rule through life," he said, "to keep the head warm, whatever happens."'

'No singing "God save the King", neither,' said the other bell-topper. 'Let your conduct be noble, and never sing the National Anthem to people wearing bell-toppers.'

'In fact,' said the first bell-topper, 'all we say is, hand over the Puddin' with a few well-chosen words, and all ill-feeling will be dropped.'

Bill was so enraged at this suggestion that he dashed his hat on the ground and kicked it to relieve his feelings. 'Law or no law,' he shouted, 'I call on all hands to knock them bell-toppers off.'

All hands made a rush for the bell-toppers, who

shouted, 'An Englishman's hat is his castle,' and 'Top-hats are sacred things'; but they were overpowered by numbers, and their hats were snatched off. 'THE PUDDIN'-THIEVES!' shouted the company.

Those bell-toppers had disguised that snooting, snouting scoundrel, the Possum, and his snoozing, boozing friend the Wombat! There was an immense uproar over this discovery, Bill and Sam flapping and snout-bending away at the puddin'-thieves, the puddin'-thieves roaring for mercy. Ben denounced them as bag snatchers, and Bunyip Bluegum expressed his indignation in a fine burst of oratory, beginning:

'Base, indeed, must be those scoundrels, who, lost to all sense of decency and honour, boldly assume the outward semblance of worthy citizens, and, by the pretentious nature of their appearance, not only seek the better to impose upon the noble credulity of Puddin'-owners, but, with dastardly cunning, strike a blow at Society's most sacred emblem – the pot-hat.'

The uproar brought the Mayor of Tooraloo hastening to the scene, followed by the local constable. The Mayor was a little, fat, breathless, beetle-shaped man, who hastened with difficulty owing to his robe of office being trodden on by the Constable, who ran close behind him in order to finish eating a banana in secret. He had some more bananas in a paper bag, and his face was one of those feeble faces that make one think of eggs and carrots and feathers, if you take my meaning.

'How now, how now!' shouted the Mayor. 'A riot going on here, a disturbance in the town of Tooraloo. Constable, arrest these rioters and disturbers.'

'Before going to extremes,' said the Constable, in a tremulous voice, 'my advice to you is, read the Riot Act, and so have all the honour and glory of stopping the riot yourself.'

'Unfortunately,' said the Mayor, 'in the haste of departure, I forgot to bring the Riot Act, so there's nothing else for it; you must have all the honour and glory of quelling it.'

'The trouble is,' said the Constable, 'that there are far too many rioters. One would have been quite sufficient. If there had been only one small undersized rioter, I should have quelled him with the utmost severity.'

'Constable,' said the Mayor, sternly, 'in the name of His Majesty the King, I call on you to arrest these rioters without delay.'

'Look here,' said Bill, 'you're labourin' under an error. This ain't a riot at all. This is merely two puddin'-thieves gettin' a hidin' for tryin' to steal our Puddin'.'

'Puddin'-thieves!' exclaimed the Mayor. 'Don't tell me that puddin'-thieves have come to Tooraloo.'

> 'It staggers me with pain and grief,
>   I can't believe it's true,
> That we should have a puddin'-thief
>   Or two in Tooraloo.
>
> 'It is enough to make one dumb
>   And very pale in hue
> To know that puddin'-thieves should come
>   To sacred Tooraloo.
>
> 'The Law's just anger must appear.
>   Ho! seize these scoundrels who
> Pollute the moral atmosphere
>   Of rural Tooraloo.'

'We protest against these cruel words,' said the Possum. 'We have been assaulted and battered and snout-bended by ruffians of the worst description.'

'How can Your Worship say such things,' said the Wombat, 'and us a-wearin' bell-toppers before your very eyes.'

'If you've been assaulted and battered,' said the Mayor, 'we shall have to arrest the assaulters and batterers, as well.'

'What's fair to one is fair to all,' said the Constable. 'You'll admit that, of course?' he added to Bill.

'I admit nothin' of the sort,' said Bill. 'If you want to arrest anybody, do your duty and arrest these here puddin'-snatchers.

> 'If you're an officer of the Law,
>   A constant felon-catcher,
> Then do not hesitate before
>   A common puddin'-snatcher.'

'We call on you to arrest these assaulters and batterers of people wearing top-hats,' said the puddin'-thieves;

> 'Our innocence let all attest,
>   We prove it by our hatter;
> · It is your duty to arrest
>   Not those in top-hats of the best
>   But those who top-hats batter.'

'It's very clear that somebody has to be arrested,' said the Mayor. 'I can't be put to the trouble of wearing my robes of office in public without somebody having to pay for it. I don't care whether you arrest the top-hat batterers, or the battered top-hatters; all I say is, do your duty, whatever happens –

> 'So somebody, no matter who,
>   You must arrest or rue it;
> As I'm the Mayor of Tooraloo,
> And you've the painful job to do,
>   I call on you to do it.'

'Very well,' said the Constable, peevishly, 'as I've got to take all the responsibility, I'll settle the matter by arresting the Puddin'. As far as I can see, he's the ringleader in this disturbance.'

'You're a carrot-nosed poltroon,' said the Puddin' loudly. 'As for the Mayor, he's a sausage-shaped porous plaster,' and he gave him a sharp pinch in the leg.

'What a ferocious Puddin',' said the Mayor, turning as pale as a turnip. 'Officer, do your duty and arrest this dangerous felon before he perpetrates further sacrilegious acts.'

'That's all very well, you know,' said the Constable, turning as pale as tripe; 'but he might nip me.'

'I can't help that,' cried the Mayor, angrily. 'At all costs I must be protected from danger. Do your duty and arrest this felon with your hat.'

The Constable looked round, gasped, and summoning all his courage, scooped up the Puddin' in his hat.

'My word,' he said, breathlessly, 'but that was a narrow squeak. I expected every moment to be my last.'

'Now we breathe more freely,' said the Mayor, and led the way to the Tooraloo Court House.

'If this isn't too bad,' said Bill, furiously. 'Here we've had all the worry and trouble of fightin' puddin'-thieves night and day, and, on top of it all, here's this Tooralooral tadpole of a Mayor shovin' his nose into the business and arrestin' our Puddin' without rhyme or reason.'

As they had arrived at the Court House at that moment, Bill was forced to smother his resentment for the time being. There was nobody in Court except the Judge and the Usher, who were seated on the

bench having a quiet game of cards over a bottle of port.

'Order in the Court,' shouted the Usher, as they all came crowding in; and the Judge, seeing the Constable carrying the Puddin' in his hat, said severely:

'This won't do, you know; it's Contempt of Court, bringing your lunch here.'

'An' it please you, My Lord,' said the Constable hurriedly, 'this here Puddin' has been arrested for pinching the Mayor.'

'As a consequence of which, I see you've pinched the Puddin',' said the Judge facetiously. 'Dear me, what spirits I am in to-day, to be sure!'

'The felon has an aroma most dangerously suggestive of beef gravy,' said the Usher, solemnly.

'Beef gravy?' said the Judge. 'Now, it seems to me that the aroma is much more subtly suggestive of steak and kidney.'

'Garnished, I think, with onions,' said the Usher.

'In order to settle this knotty point, just hand the felon up here a moment,' said the Judge. 'I don't suppose you've got a knife about you?' he asked.

'I've got a paper-knife,' said the Usher; and, the Puddin' having been handed up to the bench, the Judge and the Usher cut a slice each, and had another glass of port.

Bill was naturally enraged at seeing total strangers eating Puddin'-owners' private property, and he called out loudly:

'Common justice and the lawful rights of Puddin'-owners.'

'Silence in the Court while the Judge is eating,' shouted the Usher; and the Judge said severely –

> 'I really think you ought
>   To see I'm taking food,
> So, Silence in the Court!
> (I'm also taking port),
>   If you intrude, in manner rude,
>   A lesson you'll be taught.'

'An' it please Your Lordship,' said the Mayor, pointing to Bill, 'this person is a brutal assaulter of people wearing top-hats.'

'No insults,' said Bill, and he gave the Mayor a slap in the face.

The Mayor went as pale as cheese, and the Usher
called out: 'No face-slapping while the Judge is dining!'
and the Judge said, angrily –

> 'It's really far from nice,
>   As you ought to be aware,
> While I am chewing a slice,
>   To have you slapping the Mayor.
> If I have to complain of you again
>   I'll commit you in a trice,
>   You'd better take my advice;
>   Don't let me warn you twice.'

'All very well for you to talk,' said Bill, scornfully,
'sittin' up there eatin' our Puddin'. I'm a respectable
Puddin'-owner, an' I calls on you to hand over that
Puddin' under threat of an action-at-law for wrongful
imprisonment, trespass, and illegally using the same.'
'Personal remarks to the Judge are not allowed,'
shouted the Usher, and the Judge said solemnly –

> 'A Judge must be respected,
>   A Judge you mustn't knock,
> Or else you'll be detected
>   And shoved into the dock.
> You'll get a nasty shock
>   When gaolers turn the lock.
> In prison cell you'll give a yell
>   To hear the hangman knock.'

Here, the Usher took off his coat, as the day was
warm, and hung it on the back of his chair. He then
rapped on the bench and said –

> 'In the name of the Law I must request
> Less noise while we're having a well-earned rest.
> For the Judge and the Usher never must shirk

A well-earned rest in the middle of work.
It's the duty of both they are well aware
To preserve their precious lives with care;
It's their duty, when feeling overwrought,
To preserve their lives with Puddin' and Port.'

He sat down and tossed off a bumper of port to prove his words. 'Your deal, I think,' said the Judge, and they went on sipping and munching and dealing out cards. At this, Bill gave way to despair.

'What on earth's to be done?' he asked. 'Here's these legal ferrets has got our Puddin' in their clutches, and here's us, spellbound with anguish, watchin' them wolfin' it. Here's a situation as would wring groans from the breast of a boiled onion.'

'Why, it's worse than droppin' soverins down a drain,' said Sam.

'It's worse than catchin' your whiskers in the mangle,' said Bill.

By a fortunate chance, at this moment the Possum happened to put his snout within Bill's reach, and Bill hit it a swinging clout to relieve his feelings.

'It's unlawful,' shouted the Possum, 'to hit a man's snout unexpectedly when he isn't engaged puddin'-stealing.'

'Observe the rules,' said the Wombat solemnly. 'Be kind to snouts when not engaged in theft.'

'If it hadn't been for you two tryin' to steal our Puddin' all this trouble wouldn't have happened,' said Bill.

'It's the Mayor's fault for bringing us all here,' cried the Possum, angrily. 'If you was a just man, you'd clout him on the snout, too.'

'The Mayor's to blame,' said the Wombat. 'What about the whole lot of us settin' on to him?'

At this suggestion the Mayor trembled so violently that his hat fell off.

'What dreadful words are these?' he asked, and the Constable said hurriedly, 'Never set on to the Mayor while the local Constable is present. Let that be your golden rule.'

'That's all very well,' said Bill, 'but if you two hadn't come interferin' at the wrong moment, our Puddin' wouldn't have been arrested, and all this trouble wouldn't have happened. As you're responsible, the question now is, What are you going to do about it?'

'My advice is,' said the Constable, impressively, 'resign yourselves to Fate.'

'My advice,' said the Mayor in a low voice, 'is general expressions of esteem and friendship, hand-shaking all round, inquiries after each other's health, chatty remarks about the weather, the price of potatoes, and how well the onions are looking.'

Bill treated these suggestions with scorn. 'If any man in the company has better advice to offer, let him stand forth,' said he.

Bunyip Bluegum stood forth. 'My advice,' he said, 'is this: try the case without the Judge; or, in other words, assume the legal functions of this defaulting personage in the bag-wig who is at present engaged in distending himself illegally with our Puddin'. For mark how runs the axiom –

> 'If you've a case without a Judge,
> It's clear your case will never budge;
> But if a Judge you have to face,
> The chances are you'll lose your case.
> To win your case, and save your pelf,
> Why, try the blooming case yourself!'

'As usual, our friend here solves the problem in a few well-chosen words,' said Bill, and preparations were made at once for trying the case. After a sharp struggle, in which it was found necessary to bend the Possum's snout severely in order to make him listen to reason, the puddin'-thieves were forced into the dock. Their top-hats and frock-coats were taken away, for fear the jury might take them for undertakers, and not scoundrels. The Mayor and the Constable were pushed into the jury box to perform the duties of twelve good men and true, and the others took seats about the Court as witnesses for the prosecution.

There was some delay before the proceedings began, for Bill said, 'Here's me, the Crown Prosecutor, without a wig. This'll never do.' Fortunately, a wig was found in the Judge's private room, and Bill put it on with great satisfaction.

'I'm afraid this is unconstitutional,' said the Mayor to the Constable.

'It is unconstitutional,' said the Constable; 'but it's better than getting a punch on the snout.'

The Mayor turned so pale at this that the Constable had to thrust a banana into his mouth to restore his courage.

'Thank you,' said the Mayor, peevishly; 'but, on the whole, I prefer to be restored with peeled bananas.'

'Order in the jury box,' said Bill, sharply, and the

Mayor having hurriedly bolted his banana, peel and all, proceedings commenced.

'Gentlemen of the Jury,' said Bill, 'the case before you is one aboundin' in horror and amazement. Persons of the lowest morals has disguised themselves in pothats in order to decoy a Puddin' of tender years from his lawful guardians. It is related in the archives of the Noble Order of Puddin'-owners that previous to this dastardly attempt a valuable bag, the property of Sir Benjimen Brandysnap, had been stolen and the said Puddin'-owners invited to look at a present inside it. The said bag was then pulled over their heads, compelling the Puddin'-owners aforesaid to endure agonies of partial suffocation, let alone walkin' on each other's

corns for several hours. Had not Sir Benjimen, the noble owner, appeared like a guardian angel and undone the bag, it is doubtful if Sir Samuel Sawnoff's corns could have stood the strain much longer, his groans bein' such as would have brought tears to the eyes of a hard-boiled egg.'

'A very moving story,' said the Constable, and the Mayor was so affected that the Constable had to stuff a banana into his mouth to prevent him bursting into tears.

'I now propose to call Sir Benjimen Brandysnap as first witness for the prosecution,' said Bill. 'Kindly step into the witness-box, Sir Benjimen, and relate the circumstances ensuin' on your bag bein' stole.'

Benjimen stepped into the box, and, taking a piece of paper from his egg basket, said solemnly: 'I was very busy that morning, Gentlemen of the Jury, owing to the activity of the vegetables, as hereunder described –

'On Tuesday morn, as it happened by chance,
  The parsnips stormed in a rage,
Because the young carrots were singing like parrots
  On top of the onions' cage.

'The radishes swarmed on the angry air
  Around with the bumble bees,
While the brussels-sprouts were pulling the snouts
  Of all the young French peas.

'The artichokes bounded up and down
  On top of the pumpkins' heads,
And the cabbage was dancing the highland fling
  All over the onion beds.

'So I hadn't much time, as Your Honour perceives,
  For watching the habits of puddin'-thieves.'

'Tut, tut, Sir Benjimen,' said Bill, 'stir up your memory, sir; cast your eye over them felons in the dock, and tell the Court how you seen them steal the bag.'

'The fact is,' said Benjimen, after studying the puddin'-thieves carefully, 'as they had their backs turned to me when they were engaged in stealing the bag, I should be able to judge better if they were turned round.'

'Officer,' said Bill to Bunyip Bluegum, 'kindly turn the felons' backs to the witness.'

The Possum and the Wombat objected, saying there wasn't room enough in the witness-box to turn round, so it was found necessary to twist their snouts the opposite way.

'From this aspect,' said Ben, 'I have no hesitation in saying that those are the backs that stole the bags.'

'Make a note of that, Gentlemen of the Jury,' said Bill, and the Constable obligingly made a note of it on his banana bag.

'The identity of the bag-stealers bein' now **settled**,' went on Bill, 'I shall kindly ask Sir Benjimen to step down, and call on Sir Samuel Sawnoff to ascend the witness-box.'

Sam stepped up cheerfully, but, as the witness-box was the wrong size for Penguins, they had to hand him a chair to stand on.

'Now, Sir Samuel,' said Bill, impressively, '**I am** about to ask you a most important leadin' question.

Do you happen to notice such a thing as a Puddin' in the precinks of the Court?'

Sam shaded his eyes with his flapper and, seeing the Puddin' on the bench, started back dramatically.

'Do my eyes deceive me, or is yon object a Puddin'?' he cried.

'Well acted,' said the Mayor, and the Constable clapped loudly.

'I am now about to ask you another leadin' question,' said Bill. 'Do you recognize that Puddin'?'

'Do I recognize that Puddin'?' cried Sam in thrilling tones. 'That Puddin', sir, is dearer to me than an Uncle. That Puddin', sir, an' me has registered vows of eternal friendship and esteem.

'That Puddin', sir, an' me have sailed the seas,
Known tropic suns, and braved the Arctic breeze,
We've heard on Popocatepetl's peak
The savage Tom-Tom sharpenin' of his beak,
We've served the dreadful Jim-Jam up on toast,
When shipwrecked off the Coromandel coast,
And when we heard the frightful Bim-Bam rave,
Have plunged beneath the Salonican wave.
We've delved for Bulbuls' eggs on coral strands,
And chased the Pompeydon in distant lands.
That Puddin', sir, and me, has, back to back,
Withstood the fearful Rumty Tums' attack,

And swum the Indian Ocean for our lives,
Pursued by Oysters, armed with oyster knives.
Let me but say, e'er these adventures cloy,
I've knowed that Puddin' since he were a boy.'

'All lies,' sang out the Puddin', looking over the rim
of his basin. 'For well you know that you and old Bill
Barnacle collared me off Curry and Rice after rolling
him off the iceberg.'

'Albert, Albert,' said Bill, sternly. 'Where's your
manners: interruptin' Sir Samuel in that rude way, and
him a-performin' like an actor for your deliverance!'

'How much longer do you expect me to stay up
here, bein' guzzled by these legal land-crabs?' demanded the Puddin'.

'You shall stay there, Albert, till the case is well and
truly tried by these here noble Peers of the Realm
assembled,' said Bill, impressively.

'Too much style about you,' said the Puddin', rudely,
and he threw the Judge's glass of port into Bill's face,
remarking: 'Take that, for being a pumpkin-headed
old shellback.'

There was a great uproar over this very illegal act.
The Judge was enraged at losing his port, and the
Mayor was filled with horror because Bill wiped his
face on the mayoral hat. Sam had to feign amazement

at being called a liar, and the puddin'-thieves kept shouting: 'Time, time; we can't stand here all day.'

In desperation, Bill bawled at the top of his voice: 'I call on Detective Bluegum to restore order in the Court.'

Bunyip ran into the witness-box and, with a ready wit, shouted: 'I have dreadful news to impart to this honourable Court.'

All eyes, of course, turned on Bunyip, who, raising his hand with an impressive gesture, said in thrilling tones: 'From information received, it has been discovered that the Puddin' was poisoned at ten-thirty this morning.'

This news restored order at once. The Judge turned pale as lard, and the Usher, having a darker complexion, turned as pale as soap. The Puddin' couldn't turn pale, so he let out a howl of terror.

'Poisoned,' said the Usher, feebly. 'How, how?'

'Poisoned,' said the Judge, feeling his stomach with trembling hands. 'Until this moment I was under the delusion that a somewhat unpleasant sensation of being, as it were, distended, was merely due to having eaten seven slices. But if – '

'If,' said the Usher, in a quavering voice –

'If you take a poisoned Puddin'
  And that poisoned Puddin' chew
The sensations that you suffer
  I should rather say were due
To the poison in the Puddin'
  In the act of Poisoning You.
And I think the fact suffices
  Through this dreadfulest of crimes,
As you've eaten seven slices
  You've been poisoned seven times.'

'It was your idea having it up on the bench,' said the Judge, angrily, to the Usher. 'Now,

  'If what you say is true,
  That idea you'll sadly rue,
  The poison I have eaten is entirely due to you.
  It's by taking your advice
  That I've had my seventh slice,
  So I'll tell you what I'll do
  Why, I'll beat you black and blue,'

and with that he hit the Usher a smart crack on the head with a port bottle.

'Don't strike a poisoned man,' shouted the Usher; but the Judge went on smacking and cracking him with the bottle, singing –

  'The emotion of pity
    Need never be sought
  In a Judge who's been poisoned
    By Puddin' and Port.'

In desperation, the Usher leapt off the bench, and landed head first in the dock, where he stuck like a sardine.

'Too bad, too bad,' shouted the puddin'-thieves. 'Crowding in here where there's only room for two.' Before they could get rid of the Usher, the Judge bounded over the bench and commenced whacking them with the bottle, singing –

> 'As I find great satisfaction
>   Hitting anybody who
> Can offer that distraction,
>   Why, I'll have a go at you,'

and he went on bounding and whacking away with the bottle, while the puddin'-thieves kept roaring, and the Usher kept screaming. The uproar was deafening.

'Just listen to it,' said Bill, in despair. 'I'd like to know how on earth we are going to finish the case with all this umptydoodle rumpus going on.'

'Why,' said Bunyip, 'the simpler course is not to finish the case at all.'

'Solved, as usual,' said Bill and, seizing the Puddin' from the bench, he dashed out of Court, followed by Sam, Ben, and Bunyip Bluegum.

As they ran they could hear the Judge still whacking away at everybody, including the Mayor, and the Constable, whose screams were piercing. 'Indeed,' said Bunyip –

> 'I rather think they'll rather rue
> The haste with which they sought to sue
> Us, in the Court of Tooraloo.
> For, mark how just is Fate!

> 'The whole benighted, blooming crew,
> The Puddin'-thieves, the Usher too,
> Are being beaten black and blue
> With bottles on the pate.

> 'I rather think they will eschew,
> In future, Puddin'-owners who
> Pass through the simple rural view
> About the town of Tooraloo.'

'And now,' said Bill, when they had run a mile or two beyond the town, 'and now for some brilliant plan, swiftly conceived, which will put a stop to this Puddin'-snatchin' business for ever. For the point is,' continued Bill, lowering his voice, 'here we are pretty close up to the end of the book, and something will have to be done in a Tremendous Hurry, or else we'll be cut off short by the cover.'

'The solution is perfectly simple,' said Bunyip. 'We have merely to stop wandering along the road, and the story will stop wandering through the book. This, too, will baffle the puddin'-thieves, for while we wander along the road, our Puddin' is exposed to the covetous glances of every passing puddin'-snatcher. Let us, then, remove to some safe, secluded spot and settle down to a life of gaiety, dance, and song, where no puddin'-thief will dare to show a sacrilegious head. Let us, in fact, build a house in a tree. For, mark the advantages of such a habitation –

> 'Up on high
> No neighbours pry
>   In at the window,
> On the sly.
>
> 'Up in a tree
> You're always free
>   From bores and bailiffs,
> You'll agree.
>
> 'Up on high
> Bricks you shy
>   At bores and bailiffs
> Passing by.
>
> 'Up in the leaves
> One never grieves
>   Over the pranks
> Of puddin'-thieves.
>
> 'If you would be
> Gay and free,
>   Take my tip and
> Live in a tree.'

134

'We will, we will,' shouted the Puddin'-owners; but the Puddin' said sourly: 'This is all very well, all this high falutin'. But what about the dreadful news of being poisoned at ten-thirty this morning?'

'You ain't poisoned, Albert,' said Bill. 'That was only a mere *ruse de guerre*, as they say in the noosepapers.'

'A what?' demanded the Puddin', suspiciously.

'Let words be sufficient, without explanation,' said Bill, severely. 'And as we haven't time to waste talkin' philosophy to a Puddin', why, into the bag he goes, or we'll never get the story finished.'

So Puddin' was bundled into the bag, and Bill said, hurriedly: 'Brilliant as our friend Bunyip had proved himself with his ready wit, it remains for old Bill to suggest the brightest idea of all. Here is our friend Ben, a market gardener of the finest description. Very well. Why not build our house in his market garden. The advantages are obvious. Vegetables free of charge the whole year round, and fruit in season. Eggs to be had for the askin', and a fine, simple, honest feller like Ben, to chat to of an evening. What could be more delightful?'

Ben looked very grave at this proposal and began: 'I very much doubt whether there will be enough bed clothes for four people, let alone the carrots are very nervous of strangers – ' when Bill cut him short with a hearty clap on the back.

'Say no more,' said Bill, handsomely. 'Rough, good-humoured fellers like us don't need apologies, or any social fal-lals at all. We'll take you as we find you. Without more ado, we shall build a house in your market garden.'

And, without more ado, they did.

The picture overleaf saves the trouble of explaining how they built it, and what a splendid house it is. In

order that the Puddin' might have plenty of exercise, they made him a little Puddin' paddock, whence he can shout rude remarks to the people passing by; a habit, I grieve to state, he is very prone to.

Of course, at night they pull up the ladder in case a stray puddin'-thief happens to be prowling around. If a friend calls to have a quiet chat, or to join in a sing-song round the fire, they let the ladder down for him.

And a very pleasant life they lead, sitting of a summer evening on the balcony while Ben does his little market-garden jobs below, and the Puddin' throws bits of bark at the cabbages, and pulls faces at the little pickle onions, in order to make them squeak with terror.

On winter nights there is always Puddin' and hot coffee for supper, and many's the good go in I've had up there, a-sitting round the fire.

I didn't mean to let on that I knew their address, on account of so many people wanting to have a go at the Puddin'. However, it's out now.

When the wind blows and the rain comes down, it's jolly sitting up aloft in the snug tree-house, especially when old Bill is in good form and gives us the *Salt Junk Sarah*, with all hands joining in the chorus.

'Oh, rolling round the ocean,
From a far and foreign land,
May suit the common notion
That a sailor's life is grand.

'But as for me, I'd sooner be
A-roaring here at home
About the rolling, roaring life
Of them that sails the foam.

'For the homeward-bounder's chorus,
Which he roars across the foam,
Is all about chucking a sailor's life,
And settling down at home.

'Home, home, home,
That's the song of them that roam,
The song of the roaring, rolling sea
Is all about rolling home.'